Right Side Up

Adventures in Chelm

by Eric A. Kimmel

Illustrated by Steve Brown

APPLES & HONEY PRESS

For Lowell Cohn,

"For this you went to Stanford?"

— EAK

To Alison, Harry, Megan and Carmela,

for everything you are

— SB

Apples & Honey Press
An imprint of Behrman House
Millburn, New Jersey 07041
www.applesandhoneypress.com

Text copyright © 2019 by Eric A. Kimmel
Illustrations copyright © 2019 by Behrman House

ISBN 978-1-68115-548-7

Library of Congress Cataloging-in-Publication Data
Names: Kimmel, Eric A., author. | Brown, Steve, 1977- illustrator.
Title: Right side up : adventures in Chelm / by Eric A. Kimmel ; illustrated by Steve Brown.
Description: Millburn, New Jersey : Apples & Honey Press, an imprint of Behrman House, [2019] | Summary: An illustrated, modern retelling of collection of twelve Wise Men of Chelm stories.
Identifiers: LCCN 2018050179 | ISBN 9781681155487 (alk. paper)
Subjects: LCSH: Chelm (Lublin, Poland)—Juvenile fiction. | Children's stories, American. | CYAC: Chelm (Lublin, Poland)—Fiction. | Jews—Fiction. | Short stories.
Classification: LCC PZ7.K5648 Rig 2019 | DDC [Fic]—dc23
LC record available at https://lccn.loc.gov/2018050179

Design by Anne Redmond
Edited by Dena Neusner
Printed in China

1 3 5 7 9 8 6 4 2

022029.4K1/B1416/A8

Contents

Jacob

Simon's
Mother

Simon

Jonah

Raizel

Noah

Fonya

Zelig

Rabbi
Devora

Yossi

Right Side Up

Adventures in Chelm

Goldie · Motke · Bayla Shayna · Zakkai · Malka the Mayor · Yente · Innkeeper Mirele · Eve · Adam

ONE

The Sack of Fools

No doubt you've heard of Chelm, the town of fools. This is not to say that all fools live in Chelm. Not at all! Foolish people are all around us. Every country, every town, every village has its share of foolish people. Some rise high in the world, becoming kings, presidents, and celebrities. A few might be living in your house. Don't believe me? Look around the dinner table some night. Better yet, look in the mirror. They're everywhere.

Yet it must be said that Chelm is unusual. One tiny town having so many foolish people living in it defies the odds. How could that be?

A good question. And whenever a good question is asked, there is always a good story to answer it.

In the beginning of things, God created all kinds of souls. There were gentle souls and wicked souls, generous souls and selfish souls, peaceful souls and quarrelsome souls. Every kind of soul you can think of. Among these hundreds and millions of souls were wise souls and foolish souls.

God put the different souls in sacks. Then God called the angels and said to them, "Take these sacks and spread the souls throughout the world. Let different kinds of souls be found in every family, every community, every nation. The kind souls will balance out the wicked souls; the generous souls will balance out the selfish ones; the graceful ones will balance out the clumsy ones. The world will be in balance."

The angels took the sacks filled with souls and set about their task. They did a good job for the most part. However, the angel carrying the sack of foolish souls got caught in a storm flying over the mountains. The sack caught on a tall peak and tore open, spilling out all the souls that were inside.

The foolish souls landed in one place.

That place was Chelm. Which explains how so many foolish souls came to live there.

So they say.

❧

But they tell the story differently in Chelm. The sack the angel carried wasn't filled with foolish souls at all. It was filled with wise souls. And not just ordinary wise souls. These were the wisest of the wise.

Now among the wise souls was one very young soul. Being wise, she was not about to let herself be carried around like a load of potatoes to who-knows-where.

"Where are we going?" she asked.

None of the other souls, as wise as they were, could answer. Nobody knew.

"Well, we'd better find out," the young soul said. "The angel could drop us in the desert. Or in the ocean."

The young soul found a tiny rip in the sack. She peeked through. "What do you see?" the other souls asked.

"I see mountains. And forests. There's a river. And fields of sunflowers. It's lovely. I'd like to live here."

"Let us see!" The other souls wanted a glimpse too. They began crowding together, pushing and tearing at the hole in the sack.

RIIIIIIPPPP!!!!

The sack tore open. The souls fell out. Down, down they tumbled until—THUMP—they landed in one place.

That place was Chelm.

Which is why, the people of Chelm say, "We are all so wise that nobody else can understand us." What do most people say when they run into something they don't understand? They say, "Oh, that's foolish!"

That's how Chelm became known as the town of fools.

But the people of Chelm know better. And so do we.

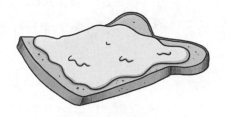

TWO

Right Side Up

Simon, Jacob the tailor's boy, was playing in the street with his friends. He was hungry, and he didn't want to go back into the house, so he asked his mother to throw him a piece of bread and butter. She buttered a piece of bread and tossed it out the window to Simon. Simon wasn't such a good catcher. The buttered bread slipped between his hands and landed in the street.

This is where the story gets interesting.

Everybody knows that when you drop a piece of buttered bread, it lands with the buttered side down. It always lands that way. You can drop a piece of buttered bread a thousand times, and it will land with the buttered side down every time. Except this time. This time a piece of bread landed with the buttered side up.

Simon and his friends stared. People in the street gathered around to look. Had cell phones been invented, they would have taken pictures of the bread to post on social media and share with their friends. They would have taken selfies with it. For this was a truly remarkable event. Never in the entire history of Chelm—maybe even in the history of the world—had a piece of buttered bread landed with the buttered side up.

How extraordinary was that? It was as if the sun rose in the west and set in the east. As if Hanukkah came in summer and Passover in the autumn. Not only had that piece of bread fallen upside down—it had turned the whole world upside down with it. If you cannot be sure that a piece of buttered bread will land the right way, what can you be sure of?

Nothing!

There had to be a reason why something that had never been known to happen happened. That was the only way to set the universe right. The town council, made up of the wisest people in Chelm, gathered to find an answer.

"It seems to me," said Bayla Shayna, "that the bread was buttered wrong. There was too much butter on one side and not enough on the other. That threw off the balance, so that when the bread fell, it landed the wrong way." Bayla Shayna was the oldest woman in Chelm and certainly the wisest. She was old enough to remember when Napoleon marched his army through Chelm on the way to Russia. Considering what happened to him in Russia, he should have stayed in Chelm. "We tried to warn him, but he wouldn't listen," said Bayla Shayna. "And they say the people of Chelm are foolish!"

"I think it was the bread, not the butter," said Adam. Adam and his wife Eve were in charge of Chelm's steam bath. Adam and Eve weren't their real names. Everyone called them that because they went around with hardly more clothes than Adam and Eve wore in the Garden of Eden. Because they worked all year round in the hot, steamy bathhouse, they dressed as if they were at the beach. Even in the dead of winter. They were very clean people because they took several baths a day. Their clothes were always clean because they hardly ever wore them. They looked good and smelled good. When you look good and smell good and wear clean clothes, people naturally think you're smart. It isn't always true, but that's how people think.

"My husband is right," Eve agreed. "Simon's mother must not have been holding the knife straight when she cut the bread from the loaf. There was too much on one side and not enough on the other. That would have thrown off the balance no matter how much butter she put on it. That's why the bread landed on the wrong side."

The members of the town council argued back and forth. Simon got bored and asked his mother to make him another piece of bread. This time he went into the house to get it. He didn't want to take the chance of it falling wrong side up again.

Seven days and seven nights passed. The town council still had not reached a decision. Finally, at noon on the seventh day, Jonah the blacksmith stood up to speak.

Now Jonah was not as old as Bayla Shayna. He was not as clean as Adam and Eve. He did not smell good. His clothes were full of holes and streaked with ashes and soot from the forge. His clothes never got clean, no matter how many times he washed them. Jonah himself was streaked with soot and ash. He never got clean

either, no matter how long he sat in the steam bath. But Jonah understood the secrets of fire and metal. He knew just how and when to strike a lump of iron to turn it into a horseshoe, a door hinge, a wagon wheel, or a pair of scissors. That automatically made him one of the wisest people in Chelm, especially since most people who consider themselves clever and wise don't know how to do anything.

"I have been listening to what others have said," Jonah began. "They have put forward many interesting ideas and ways of explaining why the bread fell on the wrong side. However, I remember someone telling me once that when there are many ways of explaining why something happens, the best answer and most likely the right answer is the simplest answer."

"And what is that?" Malka the mayor asked. Malka had been mayor for a long time. Her husband Berel had been mayor before her. When he died, the people of Chelm elected Malka to take his place. Why not? She'd been telling Berel how to run the town for years. All that changed was that Malka now sat in the mayor's chair.

Jonah stopped to clear his throat and have a drink of water. "Simon's mother was in a hurry. She didn't look to see which side of the bread she was buttering. She buttered it on the wrong side. That's why it fell with the buttered side up."

The group sat stunned. Of course! The answer was simple. The bread was buttered on the wrong side. Why hadn't they thought of that? "You're a genius, Jonah," they all said.

"It was nothing," said Jonah. He was a very modest man.

On that day the town council of Chelm passed a law. From that day on, all bread in Chelm must be buttered on the right side, so as to prevent it falling in the street wrong side up. Jonah must have been right, because from then on not a single piece of buttered bread ever landed in the street with the buttered side up.

Either that—or the children of Chelm learned to catch.

THREE

When It Snows in Chelm

Did you ever see a newspaper? Do you know what a newspaper is? Back in ancient times—well, maybe not as ancient as pyramids and painting pictures on the walls of caves, but definitely a long, long time ago— before there were laptops and tablets and cell phones and the internet, people learned what was going on in the world by reading newspapers. Newspapers were folded sheets of paper with the news of the day printed on them. Real paper! Real ink! Imagine that!

Boys and girls made money delivering these folded paper newspapers. They'd load the papers on their bicycles early in the morning, before they went to school, and ride around tossing newspapers onto front porches and

doorsteps so that people could read the news and know what was going on, good or bad, before they went to work.

Delivering newspapers was a good job. You had to be reliable and responsible to do it. Many girls and boys who delivered newspapers went on to become hugely successful. Some even became president.

They didn't have anything like that in Chelm. First of all, Chelm didn't have a newspaper. Second, nobody had a bicycle. Third, nobody was interested in reading the news anyway. Nothing in Chelm ever changed, so what was the point?

However, there was a job that was similar to delivering newspapers. This was the *shulklapper*. That means the "synagogue knocker."

The girl or boy who had the job would get up early in the morning—and I'm not talking just about Shabbat. I mean EVERY morning, no matter what the weather—and walk around town knocking on doors and shutters with a wooden mallet.

"Wake up! Wake up! It's time for morning prayers!"

People would get dressed and hurry to the synagogue for the morning service. Then they would start their day.

So you see, the *shulklapper* had an important job. The *shulklapper* was Chelm's alarm clock.

When this story begins, Raizel, the daughter of Jonah the blacksmith, had the *shulklapper* job. Raizel was a big girl. She was nearly as tall as her father and just as strong. She helped him out at the forge, hammering and banging away at glowing metal all day. Raizel was a good *shulklapper*. Nobody stayed asleep when she came around. The whole house shook when she pounded on the shutters. And when she called out, "Wake up! Wake up! It's time for morning prayers!" people heard her over in the next town.

There was just one problem. It happened the first winter Raizel took the job. Snow covered the whole town with a blanket of white. It's hard to imagine anything more beautiful than snow in Chelm. Delicate flakes drifted down from the sky, turning muddy streets, patched roofs, and everything worn-out and broken into a sparkling fairyland of frozen wonder.

But no one got to enjoy any frozen wonder. There wasn't much wonder left to enjoy.

Not after Raizel finished making her rounds. A big girl in heavy boots tromping from house to house, banging on doors and shutters, she trampled the soft white drifts as if a snowplow had gone through them.

It wasn't long before people started complaining.

"We can't enjoy the snow anymore!" said Adam and Eve. Everyone else agreed.

"We put up with ice and freezing cold all winter long. We can't do anything about that. At least let us enjoy the beauty of the snow while it's still fresh," said Bayla Shayna.

"It's not Raizel's fault," said Jonah, defending his daughter. "She has to go from house to house. How else can she do her job? What do you want her to do? Fly?"

Malka the mayor called for order. "That's not a bad idea. If Raizel's feet didn't touch the ground, she wouldn't disturb the snow."

"How is she going to do that?" sniffed Bayla Shayna. "Jonah's right. She's not a bird."

"There must be a way," said Malka. She called the Chelm town council into a special session to study the problem. They argued back and forth for seven days and seven nights until—at last!—they reached a solution.

The next time it snowed, four strong men would pick up the big oak table used for council meetings and carry it to Jonah's house. Raizel would get on the table. The men would carry the table and Raizel from house to house, so she could wake everyone up in time for morning prayers. Raizel's feet would never touch the ground. The freshly fallen snow would not be disturbed.

The idea was good. Unfortunately, like many good ideas, it didn't work. Not only didn't it work, it was a disaster! The snow was trampled worse than before. There was hardly anything left but muddy slush.

The town council called another meeting to find out what had gone wrong.

"Maybe we should fire Raizel and hire Simon again," Bayla Shayna suggested. "Simon was a good *shulklapper.*"

"Not in winter!" said Rabbi Devora. "Simon was too small. He kept getting stuck in the snowdrifts. How many times did we have to rescue him?"

Rabbi Devora was Chelm's chief and only rabbi.

Are you surprised that Chelm's rabbi was a woman? Why not? Chelm already had a woman mayor. Besides, Devora's father had been chief rabbi before her, and her grandfather before him, all the way back to the beginning of the town. Who else would they choose to be rabbi? Some stranger? Forget that!

Rabbi Devora was the wisest person in Chelm. When she spoke, everybody listened.

"Why don't we ask Raizel? She's a smart girl," Rabbi Devora suggested. "Maybe she has some ideas."

Raizel did have an idea. A good one.

"I've been watching the weather," she told everyone. "I can tell when it's going to snow. If I call people to prayers before the snow starts falling, then the snow won't have to be disturbed."

What an excellent idea! The town council applauded. Rabbi Devora praised Raizel for her intelligence and creativity. Jonah was proud of his daughter.

So that's what happened from then on. Raizel studied the winter sky. If it looked as if snow were coming, she dropped whatever she was doing and hurried to summon people to morning prayers. This worked well. Now people could look out their windows in the morning and enjoy the beauty of the freshly fallen snow for hours. Or even days.

There was one slight difficulty. Sometimes, if Raizel thought a snowstorm was on its way, she would summon people to morning prayers in the middle of the afternoon or in the dead of night. They might find themselves saying morning prayers right after afternoon and evening prayers. Sometimes, if a real blizzard was coming, they'd say morning prayers two or three times in a row in case they were snowed in.

Some people wondered if this was proper. Would their prayers count if they weren't said at exactly the right time? They asked Rabbi Devora for a decision.

Rabbi Devora studied the holy books and came to this conclusion: "It's unusual to say morning prayers when it isn't morning," Rabbi Devora admitted. "On the other hand, we can pray at any time. God always hears our prayers, no matter when we say them. And the beautiful snow is a blessing from Heaven, so why not enjoy it?"

People in other towns may disagree. But that's how they do it in Chelm.

FOUR

Yossi Gives a Speech

Rabbi Devora's husband was Zelig the butcher. It was a good match. Rabbi Devora liked to read and study. Zelig liked to work and make money. They were both proud of their son, Yossi.

Yossi was the brightest student in the Grand Yeshiva of Chelm. Of course, he was the only student in the Grand Yeshiva of Chelm. And to tell the truth, the Grand Yeshiva of Chelm wasn't so grand. It was only a closet at the back of the Grand Synagogue of Chelm, where Rabbi Devora kept her library.

But what does that matter? Yossi knew every book in that library backward and forward. He didn't have to read the books anymore because he had learned them all by heart. Yossi would have been a brilliant student anywhere.

After all, a diamond is still a diamond, whether it sits by itself in a royal crown or is mixed up with all kinds of stones in a bucket of pebbles.

Yossi's bar mitzvah was approaching. His parents wanted him to do something special, something that would be talked about in Chelm for years to come. After all, he came from an ancient rabbinical family. People had high expectations of him.

They would not be disappointed. Rabbi Devora decided that Yossi would give a *d'var Torah*, a learned lecture about the Torah reading of the week.

Rabbi Devora and Yossi spent weeks preparing the speech. They included references to all the holy books as well as the writings of a dozen famous rabbis. Such a *d'var Torah* would have been a masterpiece anywhere. Here in Chelm it was as if Moses himself had come down from Mount Sinai to deliver it.

There was one slight problem. Yossi was a nervous boy. He would freeze up if he became too anxious.

"Don't worry, Yossi. You'll be fine," his father said.

Yossi wasn't so sure.

The day of Yossi's bar mitzvah arrived. The Grand Synagogue of Chelm was packed. Everyone in town had come to hear Yossi's speech.

Yossi got through the Torah reading and the Haftarah without any problems. He could read the Bible as easily as most kids read comic books.

Giving a speech was another story. White-faced with fright, Yossi stepped up to the *bimah*. He looked out over the congregation. He opened his mouth . . .

And nothing came out. His mind suddenly went blank. The speech he and his mother had so carefully prepared, and which he had spent so many hours learning, was as gone from his brain as if someone had highlighted it and hit "DELETE."

"Yossi, we're waiting. Say something!" Rabbi Devora said.

"Go on. You can do it," said his father, Zelig, in a whisper that could be heard in the back rows of the synagogue.

Yossi, trembling, managed to squeak out a few words. "People of Chelm, family and friends, do you know what I'm going to say?"

Everyone answered with one voice: "No. We don't know what you're going to say."

Yossi sighed. "Well, neither do I."

He sat down, and that was the end of that.

Disappointing, certainly. But Rabbi Devora was not about to give up. "Try again next week," she told Yossi. "You don't have to be nervous. We're all your friends."

"But next week we read a different Torah portion," Yossi said.

"So what?" said Zelig. "Wisdom is still wisdom, even if it is a week late. Just give your speech. If anyone laughs, I'll smash him to pieces," Zelig said. He meant it.

Once more, the next week, Yossi stepped up to the *bimah*. He looked at the people in the synagogue and stammered, "People of Chelm, family and friends, do you know what I'm going to say?"

Rabbi Devora nodded to the congregation. Zelig looked around. Earlier in the week he had told everyone who came to the butcher shop what to do to give Yossi confidence.

"Yes," they all said. "We know what you're going to say."

"Oh," said Yossi. He paused, surprised. Then he said, "Well, if you already know what I'm going to say, there's no point in me saying it."

And he sat down again.

The third Shabbat came. Rabbi Devora was determined that Yossi would give his *d'var Torah* this time. Again, Zelig coached the congregation in advance.

"Yossi gets nervous. We need to make him feel confident. He'll be fine once he gets started."

So when Yossi stepped up to the *bimah* and said, "People of Chelm, do you know what I'm going to say?" some answered, "Yes, Yossi. We know what you're going to say."

And others answered, "No. We don't know what you're going to say."

Yossi paused, looked around, took a deep breath, then finally said, "I see that some know what I'm going to say and some don't. Let those who know tell those who don't. And I'll sit down."

And he did.

Rabbi Devora was disappointed. So was Zelig. Yossi was relieved. But all was not lost.

Afterward, everyone who was there agreed that Yossi gave the finest *d'var Torah* anyone had ever heard. Nobody could recall what he said, but what did that matter? Rabbi Devora's father, Rabbi Noam, had sometimes talked for hours without anyone remembering what he had said. And Rabbi Noam was the most brilliant rabbi in Chelm's long history. At least Yossi's speech was short.

And that's how they give a *d'var Torah* in Chelm.

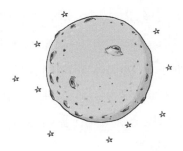

FIVE

The Moon in Chelm

The people of Chelm loved the moon. On nights when the moon was full, they brought chairs and benches into the street. They sat for hours, looking up at the moon, wondering if there were people up there looking down at them. What if there were another Chelm on the moon? Would it be like the one on earth?

What about the planets? Maybe there was a planet out there, way beyond the solar system: a planet Chelm! Why stop there? There might be a Chelm galaxy. A Chelm universe! Space aliens from Chelm zipping around the cosmos in flying saucers!

Now that was something to think about.

There was another reason why the people of Chelm loved the moon. There were no streetlights in Chelm. When the moon was dark, there was no light at all. Nobody went out at night. If they did, they stumbled around as if—well, as if they were on the dark side of the moon. Or on the far end of the universe. On planet Chelm.

"Wouldn't it be nice if we could have the moon with us every night?" Jonah the blacksmith said with a sigh. "Why does it have to go away?"

"What if it didn't go away?" said Jacob the tailor. "What if we could catch the moon and keep it here in Chelm? Then we wouldn't have to wander around in the dark. Our streets would be lit up with light like London or Paris."

"That's easy to say," said Raizel, Jonah's daughter. She was a practical girl. "How do you propose to catch the moon when it's up in the sky and we're down here on earth?"

"Let's think about this," said Jonah. "I like to go fishing. The fish are in the water. I'm on land. How do I catch them? I get them to come to me. I bait my hook. When they bite, I pull them in."

"You're going to catch the moon with fishhooks and worms?" said Raizel. "Be serious, Papa."

Rabbi Devora interrupted. "Think for a minute. Jonah's onto something. The moon isn't always up in the sky. Sometimes it comes down to earth. We can all see the moon in Lake Chelm on a clear night. It must come down to drink. What if it came down one night . . . and we caught it!

Then we'd have the moon in Chelm. We'd have moonlight whenever we wanted it."

"How are we going to catch the moon in Lake Chelm?" asked Bayla Shayna. "I'm old enough to have heard some crazy ideas, but I've never heard one as crazy as that."

"It's not crazy," said Jonah. "We don't need to bait a hook. I have a fishing net. When the moon comes down to drink, we'll throw the net over it and catch it!"

"Hmmm," said Raizel. "It could work. Let's try it and see."

The next night the moon was at its fullest. The people of Chelm dragged Jonah's fishing net down to the lake. They spread out the net, then hid in the reeds.

"Can you see it? Did the moon come down yet?" Raizel asked her father.

Jonah poked his head above the reeds. He saw the full moon reflected in the water.

"Yes! It's here! Everybody get ready. One . . . two . . . three!"

The people of Chelm flung the net. "We caught the moon! We caught the moon!" they cried.

But when they pulled the net out of the water, the moon was nowhere to be found.

"Where did the moon go?" Jonah asked.

"Up there." Raizel pointed to the sky. "We were too slow. The moon got away."

Everyone looked up. The bright full moon filled the sky overhead.

"The moon is too quick for us. We need a better plan," Jacob said.

"Maybe we need better bait," said Rabbi Devora. "The moon may come down for a drink of water. But the moon can find water anywhere. We need to find something that would make the moon want to come down and stay awhile. Something it couldn't find in every river, lake, or pond."

"How about latkes?" Eve suggested.

"It isn't Hanukkah," said Adam.

"Hamantashen?" Raizel suggested.

"It's not Purim," said Mayor Malka.

"I know," said Bayla Shayna. "Borscht! Beet soup! You can make borscht any day of the year. My great-granddaughter Goldie makes the best borscht you've ever tasted. Let Goldie make some of that borscht of hers and I tell you—the moon is ours!"

Bayla Shayna went to talk to Goldie the next morning. Goldie was glad to help. So were all the girls and boys in Chelm. Goldie and her friends spent three days making thick, rich, beet soup. Let me tell you, this was no ordinary borscht. This was borscht fit for a king. The finest restaurants in London and Paris never served borscht like this.

The manna that God sent to the children of Israel when they wandered around in the desert for forty years was a bunch of stale crackers compared to this borscht.

If anything could lure the moon down from the sky, it was Goldie's borscht. And not only the moon! Add the stars and the planets. That's how good it was.

Goldie and her friends made enough borscht to fill a barrel. Then they dumped three pails of sour cream into the barrel to make the borscht taste even better. Raizel carried the barrel to Chelm's main square. She was the only one strong enough to lift it. Everyone waited for the moon to rise.

"Can you see the moon yet?" Jonah asked Raizel. Raizel raised her head. She peered over the lip of the barrel.

"No. Not yet," she said.

They waited.

"Can you see it now?"

Raizel looked again. "No. Not yet."

They waited some more.

"Is it there yet?"

Raizel looked for a third time. This time she saw the bright full moon reflected on the surface of the borscht. "It's here. In the barrel," she whispered to everyone. "Get ready. One . . . two . . . three!"

Everyone jumped to their feet. Raizel slammed the lid on the barrel. Jonah nailed it down with hammer and nails to make sure the moon didn't escape. Together the people of Chelm joined hands and danced a merry hora around the barrel.

"We caught the moon! We caught the moon!"

Soon all of Chelm was dancing and singing.

"We caught the moon! The moon's in Chelm!"

Before they went to bed that night, the people of Chelm rolled the barrel to the synagogue. Jonah and Zelig carried it down to the basement. The captured moon would be safe in the basement until tomorrow night.

Mayor Malka sent letters to all the nearby towns and as many important cities as she could think of, telling people everywhere that the moon was no longer in the sky, but not to worry. The world wasn't coming to an end. The moon was safe and secure in a barrel in the basement of the Grand Synagogue of Chelm. Everyone was invited to come to Chelm to see the moon close up. The people of Chelm were eager and ready to welcome them.

Nobody paid any attention to the letters. They laughed and threw them away. Did the people of Chelm truly think they could catch the moon in a barrel? Clearly, they were setting a new record for foolishness.

Well, let them laugh. Watch the news some night and see what's going on in the world. There's more than enough foolishness to go around. And it isn't all in Chelm.

The next morning Rabbi Devora went down to the basement to take a look at the moon. She wanted to make sure it was full and healthy. She climbed down the basement stairs, pulled up the nails, and lifted the barrel lid. She peered down into the barrel.

No moon. Not even a glimmer of a moon. Not even a shadow of a moon.

Rabbi Devora let out a yell. The people of Chelm came running. Everyone asked the same question. Where was the moon? What had happened to it?

"It couldn't have escaped. I nailed down the lid with horseshoe nails," Jonah said. "When I nail something, it stays nailed."

"It couldn't have escaped through a hole. The barrel has no leaks. Look! It's still full of borscht," said Bayla Shayna.

"Maybe it sank to the bottom," said Goldie. She took a long ladle and dipped it into the barrel. The ladle came up empty. No moon.

Raizel sighed. "I think I know what happened." She pointed to the flecks of sour cream floating on the surface of the borscht. "The borscht was too hot. The moon melted."

Sure enough, the flecks of sour cream did look like bits of melted moon.

"What will we do?" Adam and Eve asked.

Rabbi Devora sighed. "What can we do? The moon is gone and that is the end of it. There is no moon in Chelm. But we have plenty of borscht. We may as well eat it."

A few weeks later Malka the mayor came running to the rabbi's house. "Rabbi! Rabbi!" she cried. "Come quickly! There's a strange light in the sky!"

Rabbi Devora went outside to look. She saw the moon shining overhead.

"What is that?" Malka asked.

"That's the moon," said Rabbi Devora. "What did you think it was?"

Mayor Malka was terribly confused. "Didn't the moon melt in the barrel of borscht?"

"Yes. So it did," the rabbi said.

"Then how can that light in the sky be the moon?"

Rabbi Devora laughed. "Oh, Malka! Don't be such a dunce! Don't you know that every month there's a new moon?"

And every month since then, Goldie and her friends make another barrel of borscht. Maybe this time they'll get lucky and catch the moon. Or maybe everyone in Chelm just wants an excuse to feast on Goldie's borscht.

Maybe they're not as foolish as some people think.

SIX

Postcards to God

It began with a postcard.

Eve's cousin Mayda sent the card from Israel. On the postcard was a picture of the Kotel, the Western Wall. The Kotel stands in Jerusalem. It is all that remains of the Holy Temple that stood in Jerusalem two thousand years ago. Everyone in Chelm gathered round to see it.

"Look at that!" exclaimed Jacob the tailor. "If that's just a wall, think of how magnificent the whole Temple must have been! King Solomon must have spent a fortune to build it."

"Solomon didn't build that wall. King Herod built it in the time of the Romans," said Mayor Malka. "Herod was a wicked man."

"Even a wicked person can do some good," said Bayla Shayna. "I remember the first Czar Nicholas. He was a wicked man, all right. Not a day went by when he didn't come up with a new way of persecuting our people."

"What good did he ever do?" asked Goldie.

Bayla Shayna smiled. "He died."

Jonah stared at the postcard. "Look at all the people standing in front of the Kotel! They can't all live in Jerusalem. If that many people ever came to Chelm, even for a week, our town would be famous. People all over the world would talk about Chelm the way they talk about . . ."

The others chimed in.

"New York!"

"Rome!"

"London!"

"Paris!"

"Borislav!"

"Who talks about Borislav?" Jonah asked.

"I do," said Jacob. "My cousins live there."

"In any case," Jonah said, "Chelm would be one of the world's great cities. And we who live here would all be celebrities. Imagine what it would be like being famous. I wouldn't have to break my back pounding iron all day."

"We wouldn't have to sit in a steam bath all day," said Adam and Eve.

"I wouldn't have to stitch and sew, stitch and sew, day and night," said Jacob.

"I wouldn't have to chop meat and pluck chickens," said Zelig the butcher.

"I wouldn't have to listen to arguments that go on without end," said Mayor Malka.

"Aren't you forgetting something? All these extra people coming to town would mean more work," said Rabbi Devora. "Who's going to do it?"

"We'll hire somebody," said Zelig. "We don't work anymore. We're celebrities!"

"Hiring people costs money," said Mayor Malka. "Where is this money supposed to come from? Solomon was the richest king on earth. So was Herod. Here in Chelm we don't have enough money to fix the streets. How are we going to roll out a red carpet when the streets are full of holes?"

"There's something else to consider," said Rabbi Devora. "If God made us famous, it would be for a reason. It can't be for us to sit around like lords and ladies while others slave away, doing our work. Such good fortune could only be for one purpose."

"What sort of purpose?" the people of Chelm asked.

"*Tikkun olam*," said Rabbi Devora.

"What's that?" asked Jacob.

"That's Hebrew. It means 'fixing the world.' Making the world a better place."

"What's to fix, except the streets, of course. I like Chelm the way it is," said Jacob.

"Chelm isn't the world," said Rabbi Devora. "Most people aren't as lucky as we are. There are wars and famine and disease all over."

"What can we do about that?" Bayla Shayna asked.

"I don't know," said Rabbi Devora. "Maybe if we all put our heads together, we can come up with an idea."

Mayor Malka called a meeting of the entire town. They spent seven days and seven nights thinking about what the people of Chelm could do to fix the world.

They came up with many good ideas.

"We could make moon borscht to feed the hungry," said Raizel.

"There isn't enough moon," said Bayla Shayna.

"There isn't enough borscht," said Goldie.

"We could open the bathhouse to poor people, so they could have a bath. We could wash their clothes while they were bathing," Adam and Eve suggested.

"We'd be washing clothes day and night," said Zelig. "Where would we hang them to dry? There would be clotheslines all over town."

Lots of good ideas. Unfortunately, none of them worked.

But in the end, they did come up with a plan that would work. What a plan it was! Guess who thought of it. Yossi! This time he wasn't shy at all.

"People don't go just to the Kotel to pray," said Yossi. "You don't have to drag yourself all the way to Jerusalem. You can pray anywhere. So what's special about the Kotel? At the Kotel people send notes to God. They write what they want on little pieces of paper and slip them between the cracks in the stones. Can't we offer something better than that?"

"Of course we can!" said Zelig. "The Kotel in Jerusalem is a ruin. Our holy wall will be a hundred times better. We'll fix up the western wall of our synagogue. We'll patch, plaster, and paint so that it looks even better than when it was built."

❧

Everyone in Chelm set to work. They patched, plastered, and put two coats of paint on the western wall of the synagogue. They had some paint left over, so they painted the northern wall as well. They would have painted the other walls, but they ran out of paint.

"Now we have two holy walls," Rabbi Devora said. "Maybe someday we'll get more paint. Then we'll have four."

"Two is enough for now," said Mayor Malka. "Jerusalem only has one holy wall. Here in Chelm we have two. Two holy walls for the price of one. What a bargain!"

The people of Chelm were congratulating themselves on their wisdom when Adam noticed something.

"We fixed up our walls. Now there are no cracks. Where will people put their notes to God?"

Everyone stopped in their tracks. This was a real problem. Why write notes to God if there was no way to send them? If there was no way to send them, why come to Chelm?

"I have the answer!" Rabbi Devora suddenly exclaimed. "We don't need cracks. Notes on bits of paper can fall out of a crack and get lost. We'll make sure the notes get to God."

"How?" asked Jonah.

"We'll provide a mailbox," Rabbi Devora said. "And postcards! With a picture of our synagogue on one side. Then people can write their message on the back and drop it in the mailbox. We'll even address it for them."

"How?" asked Eve.

"The postcards are all going to the same place, so we'll print one address on all of them. **God. Heaven.** What could be easier?" Rabbi Devora clapped her hands with excitement. "Think of it, everybody! We can't solve all the world's problems. But God can. From now on, nobody needs to be sad or hungry or frightened. Just come to Chelm, write out a postcard, and drop it in the mailbox at our Kotel. If you can't get to Chelm, send us a letter, and we'll fill out a postcard for you. God hears prayers all day, but how many postcards does God get? What if hundreds—no, thousands—of postcards started arriving in Heaven? That would really get God's attention. That would let God know it was time to fix this broken world."

The next step was to print postcards of the half-painted synagogue. They divided the space on the back in half. The left side was for messages to God. The right was for the address:

"Let's try it out," said
Bayla Shayna.

Everyone in Chelm
wrote a postcard to God
and dropped it in the
mailbox. What did they
write? How should I know?
Would I be so rude as to
read God's mail?

The mailbox was full when the postman came by.
He looked at all the postcards and scratched his head.

"What am I supposed to do with these?" he asked.

"Deliver them," said Mayor Malka.

"To God? In Heaven?"

The mayor shrugged. "Where else?"

"But they don't have any stamps."

"Why should you have to buy a stamp to send a postcard? You don't need money to send a prayer to God," said
Rabbi Devora.

The postman took the postcards and left, shaking
his head.

The people of Chelm waited for visitors to arrive
to make their town famous. It didn't happen. The only

person who came by was a blind beggar on crutches. Yossi wrote out a postcard for the poor man and dropped it in the mailbox.

Guess what happened next! A miracle! As soon as the postcard dropped in the mailbox, the blind man tore off the bandage covering his eyes. He could see again! He threw away his crutches. He could walk again!

He danced out of town, taking with him the money from the charity box that the people of Chelm gave him to help him on his way. Two hundred bobitzas.

(What's a bobitza? It's an old lady. That's what people in Chelm call money: old ladies. It's because the first paper money they ever saw had Empress Catherine's picture on it. They had never seen the empress, so they asked, "Who's the bobitza? Who's the old lady?" Some things don't change. Empress Catherine hasn't been on a bill in two hundred years, but in Chelm they still call money "bobitzas.")

It would be rude to point out that the postcard was still in the mailbox, so how could God have read it? That doesn't matter. God is God. If God wants to work miracles, God can work them.

God doesn't wait for the mailman.

That's what they say in Chelm.

SEVEN

A Riddle

We haven't met Noah the shoemaker yet. That's because he was out of town, visiting his sister Leah in the city of Lemberg. He's back now, so it's time we introduced him.

Noah had gone to Lemberg because his niece Bluma, whom he hadn't seen since she was a little girl, was celebrating her bat mitzvah. On the way to Lemberg he stopped in the town of Kolomea, where he spent the night at an inn. Kolomea's a nice town. My grandma was from there. It's famous for making prayer shawls and for a wild happy dance with lots of jumps called the *kolomeyka*. Check it out on YouTube.

Now back to the story. The innkeeper in Kolomea was a jolly sort. He played the accordion and kept his guests entertained with songs and stories. On the night that Noah

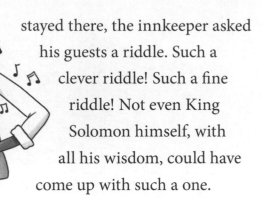

stayed there, the innkeeper asked his guests a riddle. Such a clever riddle! Such a fine riddle! Not even King Solomon himself, with all his wisdom, could have come up with such a one.

The innkeeper gathered his guests in the dining room. Then he said to them, "A bagel with lox tomorrow morning for breakfast for anyone who can guess the answer to my riddle." All the guests in the Kolomea Inn drew closer to listen. "Here's the riddle," said the innkeeper. "He's my father's son, but he's not my brother. Who is he?"

All the guests looked at each other. They rubbed their chins. They scratched their heads. They pulled their ears. Finally Noah said, "We give up. You win. What's the answer?"

The innkeeper grinned. "Listen again. He's my father's son, but he's not my brother. Who is he? It's ME, of course. Get it? I'm my father's son, but I'm not my brother."

All the guests at the Kolomea Inn laughed and laughed. Everyone agreed it was an excellent riddle. It was such a good riddle that Noah wrote it down. He didn't want to forget it. He wanted to share it with his friends when he returned home to Chelm.

Three Saturdays later, after Noah had returned from Lemberg, Rabbi Devora stepped up to the *bimah* after the Torah reading and asked if anyone had anything to ask or share for the good of the community. Noah raised his hand.

"Last month, when I was in Kolomea, I stayed at the inn. The innkeeper told us such a clever riddle. A wonderful riddle! A charming riddle! Such a riddle you don't get to hear every day! I wrote it down so I wouldn't forget. I've brought it back to Chelm to share with you. Are you ready? Listen to this." Noah unfolded the piece of paper and read the words he had written.

"He's my father's son, but he's not my brother. Who is he?"

Everyone in the synagogue, from the rabbi on the *bimah* to the children chasing each other up and down the aisles, stopped to listen. My father's son but not my brother. Who is it? Who could it be?

They scratched their heads. They rubbed their chins. They wrinkled their brows. No one could guess the answer.

"Do you give up?" Noah asked.

"Yes!" everyone in the synagogue answered.

"Then I'll tell you," said Noah. He proudly repeated the riddle: "He's my father's son, but he's not my brother. Who is he?"

"Who?"

"He's the innkeeper in Kolomea!"

And everyone laughed, for they all agreed it was an excellent riddle. The best riddle ever told in Chelm.

Even if it made no sense at all.

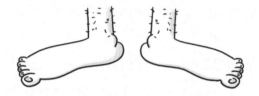

EIGHT

The Mixed-Up Feet

On hot summer days the children of Chelm loved to go swimming in Lake Chelm. They swam and dove, splashed and waded in the cool water.

One hot August afternoon Goldie and her friends were wading in the lake. They decided to have some fun. They put their arms around each other and began walking in a circle, kicking and splashing and laughing so hard they almost fell down.

Suddenly Goldie looked down at her feet. "Oh my!" she exclaimed. "We've gotten our feet mixed together. I can't tell my feet from anyone else's."

Her friends looked down too. "Goldie's right! Are those my feet or are they yours?" said Mirele.

"I don't know!" exclaimed Mirele's cousin Yente. "Our feet look alike under the water. I can't tell whose feet are whose."

Just then Simon came along. "Simon! Help!" the girls yelled.

Simon came running. "Who's drowning? I'll save them!"

"No one's drowning. But we are in trouble," said Goldie.

"Our feet are all mixed up together," Yente explained. "We don't know how to untangle them."

"We can't go home with our feet tangled up," said Mirele. "We'll have to stand here in the lake forever!" She began to cry.

"Don't cry," said Simon. "I'll figure it out." He pulled off his shoes and socks and waded into the water to help the girls. He didn't get far.

Simon looked down. "Whose feet are those? Are they mine or yours?" he asked Goldie.

"I think they're mine," Goldie said.

"No! They're mine!" said Yente.

"They're mine. They've got to be," said Mirele.

Goldie sighed. "Now Simon's feet are mixed up, too. What are we going to do! It's almost time for dinner. If we can't straighten out our feet, we'll be here all night."

"Maybe even longer!" Simon said. He shuddered, thinking of how it would be to be stuck in the frozen lake, covered with snow and ice, when winter came.

The children stood in the lake, wondering what to do, when they heard the clip-clop of hooves. It was Fonya the farmer, coming down the road on his wagon.

Fonya didn't live in Chelm. His farm was several miles outside of town. He also had far too much common sense to have been one of the souls in the angel's sack. On the other hand, he knew the people of Chelm and liked them. More importantly, he understood them.

Fonya saw the children standing in the lake. Just standing, looking frightened and sad. They weren't swimming or splashing or playing. He knew at once that something was wrong. Fonya reined in his horse. The wagon stopped in the middle of the road.

"What's the matter? Do you need help?" Fonya called to the children.

"Help us, Fonya! We're stuck!" Goldie shouted.

"How are you stuck?" said Fonya. "Is something holding you? Did you get your foot caught between some rocks? I'll come and get you out." He began pulling off his boots.

"No, Fonya! Don't come in. You'll get stuck, too," shouted Simon.

"We were playing around in the water. Somehow our feet got mixed up. We don't know whose feet are whose," Yente explained. "We can't get out of the lake if we don't have our own feet."

"We'll never get out. Never!" wailed Mirele.

Fonya shook his head. The people of Chelm never failed to amaze him. "Don't cry, dear children. I won't abandon you. I'll get you out. I know how to sort out your feet."

"How, Fonya?" the children pleaded.

"It's easy," Fonya said. He jumped up and yelled, "Boo!!!"

"YOW!" they screamed. Each one jumped back. When they did, their feet came with them.

The children ran to Fonya, hugging him. "You saved us, Fonya!"

Fonya blushed. "Oh, it was nothing. I'm happy to help. Do you need a ride back to town? Hop in the wagon. I'm going that way."

The children piled into Fonya's wagon. Back to town they went. When they got

there, they told their parents what had happened and how Fonya had rescued them.

The town council called a special meeting. They awarded Fonya a medal and a certificate to thank him for saving their children. They also made him a Knight Commander of the Order of Chelm. That allowed him to write KCOC after his name. That would have been impressive if Fonya had known how to read and write.

Unfortunately, he didn't. But he appreciated the gesture all the same.

The Chelm Town Council also considered what had happened at Lake Chelm and how their children had been plucked from disaster. They passed a law to make sure it would never happen again. From now on, all citizens of Chelm who went swimming or wading in a lake, pond, or river had to tie a label with their name on it around each ankle. That way, should their feet get mixed up, they could easily be sorted out.

That must have worked because no one's feet ever got mixed up again. Which goes to show that if you think hard enough, there's always a solution to every problem.

Especially in Chelm.

NINE

The Fools on the Hill

I t's said that God doesn't make single souls. God makes them in pairs so that every soul has a soul mate somewhere. The challenge is to find that perfect partner for whom you were created.

People firmly believe that in Chelm. Look at Bayla Shayna and her husband Naftali. They were married for fifty-seven years. Naftali died with a smile on his face because, it was said, he could look forward to spending eternity with his dear wife in Heaven. I'll admit that some rude people said he was smiling because he didn't have to listen to Bayla Shayna's nagging anymore. But pay no attention to that. Love always wins in the end. Take Goldie and Simon.

If there were ever two souls created for each other, they were Simon and Goldie. Goldie loved Simon. Simon loved

Goldie. Their parents arranged their marriage when they were infants. Even now, though they were still children, no one looked forward to their wedding more than Goldie and Simon. The two walked together in the countryside, talking about where they would like to live and how many children they would like to have.

"I want lots of children," said Goldie as she walked with Simon in the forest around Lake Chelm.

"How many?" Simon asked.

"At least eight. Maybe more," said Goldie.

Simon thought about that. "We'll need a big house for that many people. I don't know if there's a house that big in Chelm. We'll have to build one. Where shall we build it?"

"Right here," Goldie said. "By the lake. At the foot of Mount Chelm."

Mount Chelm was what they called the big hill outside of town. It wasn't really a mountain, but it was the tallest hill around, so it would have to do. Chelm isn't Switzerland, you know.

Goldie continued, "We'd have a garden. I could grow flowers and vegetables. Our children could help. We could walk beside the lake and go fishing. In winter we could go ice skating or sledding down the mountainside. What fun it would be, Simon! I can hardly wait to grow up."

Simon suddenly stopped. He pointed toward the top of the hill. "Goldie, look up there. Do you see that rock?"

Goldie looked where Simon was pointing. A boulder the size of a house rested on the hillside. She clutched Simon's hand.

"Oh, no!" she gasped. "I never noticed that rock before. It's huge! Simon, what if our dreams came true and we built our house at the foot of Mount Chelm. What if we and our children and your parents and my parents were gathered together at our table for the Passover seder and that boulder came loose and began rolling down the mountainside! What if it hit our house when we were in it!"

"We'd all be killed! Squashed flat!" Simon gasped. "All our hopes and dreams! All those precious lives! Wiped out in a moment!"

Goldie and Simon began to cry. They were still crying when their parents came to find them.

"Goldie! Simon! What's wrong?" they asked.

"Goldie and I were talking about how we would be married and have lots of children," Simon said. "We'd build a big house right here, on the shore of Lake Chelm. We'd invite everyone in our families to come to our Passover seder. Suddenly, while we were all gathered around the table . . ."

Goldie pointed up the hillside. "That big rock up there would come loose. It would roll down the hill and come crashing down on our house. We'd all be squashed flat! House! Children! Everybody!"

"Oh, no! What a tragedy!" wailed Bayla Shayna, Goldie's great-grandmother.

"Who could go on living after such a disaster!" moaned Jacob, Simon's father.

They were all moaning and wailing and crying and carrying on when Fonya came down the road in his wagon.

"Something terrible has happened!" He jumped off the wagon and came running to see how he could help.

"What's the matter?" Fonya asked.

Goldie began. "After Simon and I got married, we'd have lots of children . . ."

Simon finished. "That big stone up there on the hill would roll down and squash everyone around our seder table flat as matzah!"

Fonya shook his head.

"Listen to me, everyone. If you're scared about that big stone on the hill, get rid of it. Move it somewhere else. Then you won't have to worry about it flattening your house. Meanwhile, Goldie and Simon are still children themselves. It will be years before they have a house and children of their own. There's nothing to worry about, I tell you. Go home and forget the whole thing."

Fonya got in his wagon and drove away.

Goldie and Simon went home, but they did not forget. They talked to their friends. Mayor Malka called the town council into session to decide what to do about the dangerous rock on Mount Chelm.

The meeting went on for seven days and seven nights. A lot of good ideas were offered.

"Goldie and Simon could build their house on stilts. If the stilts were high enough, the stone would roll under the house without doing damage," said Jonah.

"We could dig a moat around the house and fill it with water from Lake Chelm. When the stone came rolling down the hill, it would tumble into the moat instead of squashing the house," suggested Zelig.

"We could get lots of glue, and glue all the stones on Mount Chelm in place, so they wouldn't roll," said Jacob.

Lots of good ideas. But in the end, everyone decided that Fonya was right. The best and easiest way to avoid a future tragedy was to move the stone. But instead of waiting years, they should move it now in case they forgot to do it later.

The people of Chelm went out to the hillside the next day. They brought ropes and crowbars, picks and shovels. They wrapped the ropes around the stone. Then they dug away the earth that was holding it in place. Finally, with half the town pushing up at the stone so it wouldn't roll too fast and the other half pulling on the ropes so it wouldn't squash the people who were pushing up at it, they slowly began lowering the stone down the hillside.

When they had the stone halfway down, Fonya came along to see what they were doing. He took one look and asked, "Why?"

"What do you mean?" the people of Chelm answered, tugging on the ropes and pushing at the stone as if their lives depended on it. Which, in fact, they did.

Fonya shook his head. "I mean, why are you going to all this trouble to move the stone? One good push and it will roll down the hill by itself. It can't hurt anything. We're in the middle of a forest. At worst it will knock over a couple of trees."

Fonya walked away, shaking his head. If there was a hard way and an easy way to do something, count on the people of Chelm to pick the hard way.

But this time the people of Chelm decided Fonya was right. Especially since they were all getting tired and wanted to go home.

"Why are we knocking ourselves out, risking our necks, trying to get this stone down the hill? All we have to do is give it a push."

So the people of Chelm, groaning, sweating, pushing on the stone and pulling on the ropes until their hands blistered, hauled the huge stone back up the hill to where it was before.

They all cheered. "We've done it! Now let's finish the job so we can go home."

The people of Chelm gathered uphill behind the stone.
"One, two, three . . . PUSH!" shouted Mayor Malka. Everyone
pushed at once. The stone began to roll, slowly at first, then
faster and faster. It bounced and rolled all the way to the
bottom of the hill, crashing into several trees and smashing
them to splinters until it finally came to a stop on the shore
of Lake Chelm.

"Hooray!" everyone shouted. Except Goldie. She stared
at the stone, shaking her head.

"Goldie, what's the matter?" said Simon.

"It's the stone. Look where it is, Simon! We were going
to build our house by the lakeshore.
Now that awful stone is where our
house is supposed to be. My
dream is ruined. I
can't bear it."

"There's only one thing to do," her friend Raizel said. Nobody had to ask what that was.

So once more they tied the ropes around the stone and, pushing and pulling, hauled it all the way up the hill to the very top.

"We're not doing this again!" said Adam.

"That's right!" Eve and everyone else agreed. They all gathered behind the stone and with one big push sent it rolling down the other side of the hill.

Except they forgot one tiny detail. They rolled the stone down the side of the hill facing Chelm. The huge stone bounced and rolled through town. Fortunately, everyone was up on the hillside or someone could easily have been squashed. What was not so fortunate was that the stone crashed into a building with a loud CRUNCH!!!

That building happened to be the synagogue.

The stone obliterated one entire wall, leaving nothing but splinters.

Rabbi Devora let out a yell. So did the rest of the people of Chelm. They came pouring down the hillside. They stood in the street, surveying the damage.

"Our beautiful synagogue, the only one in the world with two holy walls, is destroyed!" said Bayla Shayna.

"Not so fast. Don't give up yet," said Rabbi Devora. A big smile crossed her face as she walked around the synagogue. "Those postcards we sent to God must have made a difference. God protected our synagogue. Take a look. There's no real damage done. The stone knocked out one wooden wall. It didn't touch the two holy ones that we painted. The ark and the *bimah* aren't damaged. Leave the stone where it is. We'll rebuild around it. The stone will become one of our synagogue's walls."

"Who ever heard of a stone as a wall?" asked Jonah.

"Did you forget that postcard of the Kotel?" Rabbi Devora said. "What is that wall in Jerusalem but a pile of huge stones? King Solomon used huge stones to build the Temple. So did King Herod. Well, so will we. Our

synagogue will be famous. We now have three holy walls and one is a stone as big as the ones you'll see at the Kotel in Jerusalem. And we don't have to paint it!"

It didn't take long to repair the synagogue. Everyone agreed the task was a lot easier than hauling that huge boulder up and down the hill. When they finished, they were so proud that they had pictures taken with everyone in Chelm standing in front of the synagogue's new wall. Simon, Goldie, and Fonya stood in front, as they should, because none of this would have happened without them.

Soon after these events, the Chelm Town Council called a special meeting. They considered the matter of what to do in the future about dangerous stones on Mount Chelm. The discussion went on for seven days and seven nights. At last, they reached a conclusion.

From now on, they decided, all houses built in Chelm had to be built on wheels, so they could be rolled out of the way if a big rock ever came rumbling toward them.

People from other towns laughed at first. Then the idea caught on. Today houses on wheels are everywhere.

We call them RVs.

TEN

The Shofar

The Chelm Town Council was like town councils all over the world. They didn't like to spend money. Spending money meant raising taxes. Nobody, wise or foolish, ever liked that. Therefore, lots of things that needed to be done didn't get done.

Like paving the streets. Chelm's streets were a sea of mud, especially in the spring when the snow melted and the rain began falling. Everyone walked around in tall leather boots. Walking around on stilts might have been an even better idea, because some of those mudholes could easily have swallowed a horse and wagon.

"We need to do something about fixing the streets," Mayor Malka told the council. Everyone agreed. However, there was no money in the treasury. Street repair would have to wait for the following year.

("Besides," Bayla Shayna muttered to Jonah the blacksmith, "when were our streets ever paved? They're fine the way they are. They were good enough for our ancestors. They're good enough for us.")

On her way home, Bayla Shayna slipped as she was crossing the street and fell face-first in the mud. It still didn't change her thinking.

Fonya the farmer was the next victim. He had come into town to pick up supplies for the spring planting. He stepped in a mudhole as he climbed out of his wagon and sank up to his waist in mud.

"Help!" Fonya yelled.

It's good there were people around to pull him out. Otherwise, the mud would have swallowed him like quicksand. What a tragedy that would have been! As it was, the sticky mud sucked the left boot off his foot.

"My boot!" Fonya cried. The people of Chelm tried to help him. They gathered long sticks and poked around in the mud, hoping to find the boot and lift it out. No luck! Fonya's boot was as gone as if the earth had swallowed it up. Which, in a way, it had.

"When are you going to fix the streets?" Fonya grumbled.

"We're working on it," the people of Chelm told him.

But in one sense, it wasn't a complete loss. Fonya's boots had been mended so many times that if you took away the patches there would hardly have been any boot left. His wife had been nagging him for months to get new boots, so in one sense the mudhole forced him to do what he should have done long ago. Fonya headed home with a pair of sturdy new boots and a wagonload of supplies, complaining all the while about how it cost him a fortune every time he came to town.

And that would have been the end of the story. Except several months later, just before Rosh Hashanah, Yossi and Simon were tossing a ball around in the street when they noticed something sticking out of a dried-up mudhole.

"What's that?" said Yossi.

"I don't know," said Simon. "Let's find out."

They pulled and tugged. At last the object came loose. What they discovered when they washed the mud off was a stiff, curved, chocolate-brown object with a large round hole at one end and a smaller hole at the other.

A crowd had gathered by this time. Chelm's mudholes didn't often give up their secrets. Several Chelmites

ventured guesses, but no one
came close to identifying the
mysterious object.

They decided to take it
to Rabbi Devora. If anyone
could solve the mystery, it
would be her.

Rabbi Devora placed the
object on a table. She turned it this way. She turned it that
way. She turned it over and looked at it from every angle.
She raised it over her head and peered inside. Finally, she
set it down.

"I know what it is," she announced.

"What?" everyone asked.

"It's a shofar," Rabbi Devora told them. "It's hard like
a ram's horn. It's curved like a ram's horn. It has a big hole
in front where the sound comes out and a little hole in the
back to blow through. No question about it. It's a shofar."

"How did a shofar come to be at the bottom of a
mudhole in the middle of the street?"

Rabbi Devora shrugged her shoulders. "Who knows?
Maybe an angel dropped it, and it fell down from Heaven.
All I know is that it's a shofar."

"What should we do with it?" Mayor Malka asked.

"We do what we do with a shofar," Rabbi Devora
answered. "First we'll clean it. After we get out all the mud,

we'll blow it. Rosh Hashanah is coming. Let us show our appreciation for this gift from Heaven by blowing it during the shofar service."

⤫

Jonah the blacksmith was Chelm's official shofar blower. When he blew shofar the sound could be heard from one end of town to the other. And when he blew the final *tekiah gedolah*, the synagogue walls shook. But even Jonah, with all his strength and talent, found it difficult to get much of a sound out of this shofar. He tried and tried, but the most he could achieve was a leathery sound, somewhat soft and muddy.

"Are you sure this is a shofar?" he asked Rabbi Devora.

"Of course it's a shofar," Rabbi Devora insisted. "Maybe not a great shofar, but a shofar all the same."

⤫

The first day of Rosh Hashanah arrived. All of Chelm gathered at the synagogue. Every seat was filled. Even Fonya the farmer came, dressed in his best clothes and new boots. He brought his whole family. Fonya liked coming to the synagogue. He enjoyed the music even though he didn't know the words. Rabbi Devora always gave a fine sermon. And in the end there was a *kiddush* with challah and wine and plenty of other good things to eat.

As the people in the synagogue prepared for the blowing of the shofar, Fonya noticed something. He stared at the object in Jonah's hands.

"Hey! That's my boot!" he yelled.

Everyone turned around. "Shhhhh! Don't disturb the shofar blowing!"

"But that's not a shofar!" Fonya insisted. "Jonah's blowing my boot!"

Consternation filled the synagogue. Was the shofar blowing valid if the shofar blower blew a boot instead of a shofar? Such a problem would rack the brains of the greatest rabbis in history. They might argue about this issue for months, if not years.

But the people of Chelm didn't have years. Or months. They needed to blow the shofar NOW. They looked to Rabbi Devora for a decision. She did not hesitate.

"I rule that the object in question is a shofar." She turned to Jonah. "Blow!"

Jonah blew as he had never blown before. And if the sounds that came out of the shofar—or the boot—didn't exactly rattle the walls, they were still identifiable as the traditional shofar blasts.

Tekiah . . . shevarim . . . teruah . . . tekiah gedolah!

❧

When the Rosh Hashanah service ended, Fonya and the people of Chelm gathered around as Rabbi Devora examined the shofar again. She turned it this way and that. She examined it from top to bottom. Finally, she had Fonya take off his boot and attempt to pull the shofar onto his foot. It was a bit tight, as might be expected of a boot that had lain at the bottom of a mudhole for months, but it did fit.

"See!" said Fonya, pointing to a hole in the toe. "I was going to get that mended when I came into town."

Noah the shoemaker looked the boot over. "Fonya's right," he said. "I know all these patches. They're my work. It's Fonya's boot, all right."

Rabbi Devora considered the new evidence. "The facts are clear. Our shofar is indeed Fonya's old boot. But we cannot give it back to him. The boot has been used as a shofar. Once an everyday object has been used for a holy purpose, it becomes holy. It can never be used for ordinary purposes again. Thus I say that this object may have once been a boot, but it has been used as a shofar and it must remain a shofar."

Fonya frowned. "That doesn't seem right to me. It's my boot. Don't you have to give it back?"

"We do," said Rabbi Devora. "Or we can pay you its value. Let me see. The price of a good-quality shofar would be fifteen bobitzas. Let's add three more to make eighteen. That stands for *chai*: life. It will be a special blessing. Will you accept my offer of eighteen bobitzas?"

Fonya didn't hesitate. "Eighteen bobitzas? You bet!"

The people of Chelm objected. "Eighteen bobitzas for a beat-up old boot? Are you mad?" they shouted at Rabbi Devora.

Fonya laughed. "Beat-up old boot? What are you talking about? Open your eyes, my friends. It's a shofar!"

ELEVEN

The Sign

Motke the fish seller had sold fish his whole life. His father had been a fish seller before him. And his grandfather had sold fish before him.

Motke's family had been selling fish for generations. Yet they barely made a living. At least they could eat the fish they didn't sell. Otherwise, they would have starved to death.

Across the street from the fish store stood the shop of Zelig the butcher. Zelig was a huge, heavy man. Turkeys, ducks, chickens, geese, and fine cuts of meat filled the window of his shop. Zelig was a good businessman. His shop prospered. He was one of the richest men in Chelm and one of the most charitable.

ZELIG'S MEAT MARKET
BEST MEAT IN CHELM

Zelig felt sorry for his friend Motke. He wanted to help him. But Motke was a proud man. He would not accept charity. Zelig asked his wife, Rabbi Devora, what he could do. Rabbi Devora told him to wait for the right time. It was sure to come.

One day Motke asked Zelig, "How is it that you are rich and I am poor? We both sell food that is good to eat. Yet your shop is always full of customers and mine is empty. What is your secret?"

"Aha!" Zelig thought. "Here is my chance! Motke

won't accept charity, but he will accept good business advice. By helping his business, I can help him."

Zelig said to Motke, "There's no secret. Do you think it's magic? Why did you wait so long to ask me? Aren't we friends? Let's go outside. I'll gladly show you how I do it."

Zelig led Motke across the street. "Look at my shop. Do you see the big sign in front?"

How could anyone miss it? The sign said, **ZELIG'S MEAT MARKET. BEST MEAT IN CHELM**. Underneath the words were pictures of goats, sheep, ducks, and chickens.

"I advertise. That's the secret of my success," said Zelig. "When people start thinking about what they are going to eat for dinner, they see my sign and know where to go." He pointed across the street at Motke's shop. "Look at your shop. There's nothing there. If you want people to buy your fish, you have to put the idea FISH into their heads. Otherwise, they'll walk right by."

Motke nodded. "You're right. I see what my family has been doing wrong. If you want your business to be successful, you have to advertise."

"You're catching on!" said Zelig. "Put up a sign like I do. I guarantee customers will come bursting through your door."

Motke went back to his shop and got busy. He took a large board. On it he wrote in big letters:

Underneath the words he painted a picture of a salmon surrounded by a school of herring and four laughing carp. He hung the sign on the wall of his shop and waited for customers to arrive.

Bayla Shayna was the first to show up.

"Do you like my new sign?" Motke asked her.

Bayla Shayna shrugged her shoulders. "I don't understand it. Why do you need to say Motke's Fish Store? Everybody in Chelm knows it's your store and that you sell fish. Your family has sold fish in this store for generations."

Motke had to agree that Bayla Shayna was right. He went outside and painted over **Motke's Fish Store**. Now the sign read:

Underneath was a picture of a salmon surrounded by a school of herring and four laughing carp.

Noah the shoemaker came by next. He looked at the sign and said to Motke, "I don't understand your sign. Why do you have to say **Fresh Fish**? Of course they're fresh! Who sells spoiled fish? You also don't need to say **Daily**. When else are you going to sell them? If you sold them yesterday, they wouldn't be fresh. If you sold them tomorrow, they wouldn't be here. And you certainly won't sell them on Shabbat because that's when you're closed."

Noah was right. Motke painted out the words **Fresh** and **Daily**. Now the sign read:

Underneath was a picture of a salmon surrounded by a school of herring and four laughing carp.

Mayor Malka came by. She stood in the street, staring at the sign. Motke went outside to talk to her.

"What's the matter?" he asked the mayor.

Malka pointed to the sign. "Why does your sign say **Fish Sold Here**? Of course you sell fish! You don't give them away. And you obviously sell them here, in Chelm. Not in some other town. So why do you need to say that?"

Malka was right. Motke went outside and painted out the words **Sold** and **Here**.

Now the sign read:

Underneath was a picture of a salmon surrounded by a school of herring and four laughing carp.

Jonah the blacksmith was the next to come by. He looked at the sign, then at the shop, and said to Motke, "That's a strange sign. Why do you need to say **Fish**? Everyone knows you sell fish. What else do you sell in a fish store? And why do you have that picture? We can see the fish in your window. We can smell them."

Motke agreed with Jonah. He went outside and painted over the picture of the salmon, the herring, and the carp along with the word **Fish**. Now the sign read:

Underneath was a picture of . . .

Zelig walked across the street to have a look. He stared at the blank board.

"What happened to your sign?" he asked Motke.

"It had too many words. I corrected it," Motke said.

"But there's nothing on it!" Zelig said. "It's just a blank board. Why do you even bother to hang it up?"

"Because I'm no fool," Motke said, tapping his forehead. "I remember what you told me. Now I know what it takes to run a successful business. You have to advertise!"

TWELVE

Zakkai Goes to Heaven

Zakkai was the oldest person in Chelm. He was even older than Bayla Shayna. Bayla Shayna remembered Napoleon. Zakkai remembered Napoleon's father. And his grandfather.

"A nice man," Zakkai said about him. "He liked to whistle. He could imitate birdsongs."

One night, Zakkai had a dream. The Angel of Death came to him and said, "Zakkai, prepare yourself. Your days are coming to an end. You're going to die."

"So what?" Zakkai said. "That's not news. I've known that all my life. Why don't you tell me something I don't already know? Like, where am I going when I do die?"

"You've led a good life, Zakkai," the angel said. "Have no fear. You're going to Heaven."

"Wonderful! When?" Zakkai asked. "I'm ready to go now."

"Not yet," the angel told him. "There are a lot of people ahead of you. I'll be back in maybe six months, a year. . . ." Then the angel disappeared.

Zakkai woke up. "The Angel of Death wakes me up in the middle of the night, tells me my days are numbered, then doesn't tell me what the number is. What nonsense!"

Zakkai decided not to wait for the angel to come back. If he was going to Heaven, he might as well get started. The sooner he began his journey, the sooner he'd get there.

Everyone in Chelm came to see Zakkai off. They wished him a safe journey—although how safe could a journey be if he was going to die at the end of it? Zakkai promised to write after he got to Heaven. He felt sure he'd find an angel to deliver the letter. Maybe he'd be able to write back on one of God's postcards.

Zakkai wiped his eyeglasses with his handkerchief, so he could see where he was going. Then, with his walking stick in

hand, his old hat on his head, a pack on his back, and a pair of sturdy boots on his feet, he started down the road.

He walked along for a few miles without meeting a soul. That didn't bother him. "I'll meet plenty of souls soon enough, considering where I'm going," he told himself.

Eventually he came upon two boys riding bareback on an old horse. They were Fonya's sons, Ivan and Ihor.

"Hello, Grandpa Zakkai! Where are you going?" they asked. "Want a lift? You can ride our horse. We'll carry your pack."

"Thank you, boys. I can walk. It's a fine day for walking. Where am I going? I'm going to Heaven," Zakkai answered.

"Say hello to our grandma when you get there," the boys said. "Tell her we miss her."

"I'll do that. I remember your Grandma Masha. I miss her too. She was a good friend of mine."

Zakkai walked along with the boys until they came to the bridge over the River Chelm. Ivan and Ihor turned around. They needed to be home in time for dinner. Zakkai waved goodbye and walked on. He crossed the bridge and

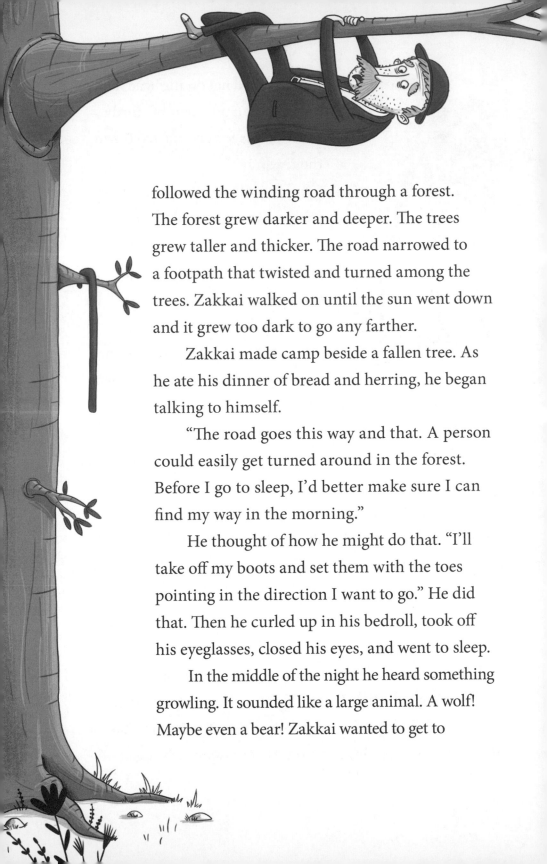

followed the winding road through a forest.
The forest grew darker and deeper. The trees
grew taller and thicker. The road narrowed to
a footpath that twisted and turned among the
trees. Zakkai walked on until the sun went down
and it grew too dark to go any farther.

Zakkai made camp beside a fallen tree. As
he ate his dinner of bread and herring, he began
talking to himself.

"The road goes this way and that. A person
could easily get turned around in the forest.
Before I go to sleep, I'd better make sure I can
find my way in the morning."

He thought of how he might do that. "I'll
take off my boots and set them with the toes
pointing in the direction I want to go." He did
that. Then he curled up in his bedroll, took off
his eyeglasses, closed his eyes, and went to sleep.

In the middle of the night he heard something
growling. It sounded like a large animal. A wolf!
Maybe even a bear! Zakkai wanted to get to

Heaven, but not that way. Frightened, he climbed a tree and hid in the branches until dawn arrived.

He climbed down to find that a large animal had indeed invaded his campsite. Everything in his backpack was strewn around. All his food had been eaten. His boots, which were supposed to point the way, had vanished. He had to hunt in the forest for most of the morning before he found them. He never did find his eyeglasses.

Zakkai gathered what was left of his belongings. His boots were chewed, but not damaged. He pulled them on his feet and considered what to do next.

"Do I go left? Do I go right?" he asked himself. It was hard to tell which way was which without his glasses. The forest trees all looked the same—blurry! Finally, he said to himself, "Since I am going to Heaven, I'll put myself in God's hands. God will show me the way even if I can't see where I am going."

He stood in the middle of the path, closed his eyes, and whirled around and around. "Show me the way, God!" he called. "Which way leads to Heaven?"

Zakkai stopped and opened his eyes. "Aha! That way!" he exclaimed, and he began walking in the direction God had shown him.

Except it wasn't the way to Heaven. The road he began following led right back to Chelm. You might think he would have noticed that, but without his eyeglasses he couldn't see two steps ahead.

❧

Guess where he ended up. Zakkai looked around.

"Hmmm," he said to himself. "This is a surprise. If I didn't know better, I'd say I was back in Chelm. Heaven looks exactly like Chelm. I thought it would be different, but I guess not. As Rabbi Devora often tells us, God does what Goes does. If God chooses to make Heaven look like Chelm, who am I to complain?"

Zakkai walked through the center of town, greeting everyone he saw. "Hello! Hello, everybody! I've come a long way. It's wonderful to finally get here."

The people of Chelm were confused at first.

"Isn't that Zakkai? Didn't he just leave for Heaven? What's he doing back?" Raizel said to her father, Jonah.

"You're right. That man does look like Zakkai. How can that be?" Jonah answered.

"It can't be," said Rabbi Devora. "Nobody ever comes back from Heaven, so that isn't Zakkai. It must be somebody who looks like him. Besides, Zakkai was nearsighted. He couldn't find his way across the street without his eyeglasses, let alone come back from Heaven."

If Rabbi Devora said it, it must be true. And she was right. Nobody ever came back from Heaven. Except, perhaps, the Prophet Elijah. But he only came around on Passover and that was many months away.

"Welcome to our town! We're glad to see you, whoever you are," the people of Chelm said. "Do you have a twin brother? You look a lot like our friend, Zakkai."

"I don't have a twin, but my name is Zakkai too. Where is this Zakkai? Does he really look like me? I'd like to meet him," Zakkai said.

"I'm sorry," said Mayor Malka. "Our friend Zakkai left us to go on a long, long journey. I doubt that he'll ever come back."

"He wore eyeglasses," said Jonah. "Do you wear eyeglasses?"

"I used to," said Zakkai. "I don't need them now. God showed me how to get here. I've heard so much about this place. I've been waiting my whole life to see it. Can you show me around?"

"Of course!" they said. Everyone was astonished that someone had spent his whole life waiting to get to Chelm. Goldie and Simon took Zakkai by the hand and gave him a tour of all the famous sites.

"This is our synagogue," said Goldie. "It has three holy walls. One is a giant stone."

"That's amazing! The synagogue in my town has three holy walls too. And one is a giant stone—just like that one," said Zakkai.

"This is my fish store," said Motke the fish seller. "The sign in front has nothing on it. I figured that I didn't need to write anything. But it's important to advertise."

"The fish store in my town has a sign just like it!" Zakkai exclaimed. "It's across the street from the butcher shop too. And the butcher looks just like you!"

"How interesting!" said Zelig the butcher.

Rabbi Devora showed him Chelm's famous shofar. "It looks like a boot. Once it was a boot. But it's a shofar now."

"So was the shofar in our town!" Zakkai gasped.

"Do you like riddles?" Noah the shoemaker asked. "I know a good one. He's my father's son, but he's not my brother. Who is he?"

"It's the innkeeper in Kolomea!"

"That's right!" said Noah. "I didn't think anyone else knew that riddle."

"It's a great riddle! We tell it all the time in our town," said Zakkai, amazed. "Even the smallest children know it."

As Goldie and Simon led him through town, Zakkai met one surprise after another. Heaven was just like Chelm. The same houses. The same shops. The same synagogue. Even the people looked the same as far as Zakkai could tell without his eyeglasses. They even told the same riddles. The streets were full of the same holes.

Zakkai began thinking. If Heaven was just like Chelm, why bother to go through the trouble of getting here? He could just as easily have stayed home. Which got him thinking some more. His friends back in Chelm needed to be told the truth about Heaven. Otherwise, they'd spend their lives longing for a place that was no better than where they lived now.

After a dinner of delicious moon borscht, Zakkai asked, "Do I have to stay here? Can I go home?"

"Sure!" Mayor Malka said. "This isn't a prison. You can leave any time you like."

"Really?" asked Zakkai.

"Really," said Rabbi Devora. "We all go back and forth as we please."

"I didn't know that," said Zakkai, still believing he was dead and in Heaven. "I thought that once you came here, you had to stay."

"Oh no!" said Mayor Malka. "It's not like that at all. People come and go as they please."

"In that case," Zakkai said, "you won't mind if I leave in the morning? I want to go home so I can tell the people in my town about you."

"Give them our regards," said Jonah the blacksmith. "Tell them that they're welcome to come here anytime. We'll be happy to see them."

Zakkai left the next morning. Since God was showing him the way, he didn't have to worry about going in the wrong direction. In the morning he got up, turned himself around and around, and started walking in the direction he was facing when he stopped.

God must have been helping him because that was exactly the way he wanted to go.

Back to Chelm.

"Hello, everybody! It's me—Zakkai! I'm back," Zakkai said.

The people of Chelm took one look and ran away screaming. "A ghost!"

"Come back! Don't be afraid. I'm not a ghost!" Zakkai called to them.

Rabbi Devora approached him cautiously. "Are you really Zakkai? You don't look like you. Where are your eyeglasses?" she asked him.

"I lost them in the forest," Zakkai said. "I don't need them anymore. God has shown me the way."

Rabbi Devora touched his hand, then his shoulder, then his face. "You are real. I can feel your flesh. How can that be? No one ever comes back from Heaven."

"That's not so. People come and go all the time. That's what they told me there," Zakkai said. "It must be true because here I am."

"That's really strange," Bayla Shayna said.

"No stranger than what happened while you were gone, Zakkai," Zelig said. "We had a visitor. He could have been your twin brother, except he didn't have eyeglasses. His name was Zakkai too. He never did say where he came from, but he told us his town was just like ours."

"His synagogue has three holy walls, and one is a huge stone," said Mayor Malka.

"They blow a shofar that looks like an old boot!" said Jonah.

"The fish store has a sign just like mine!" said Motke.

"He knew the answer to my riddle right away!" said Noah.

"Forget all that," said Bayla Shayna. "Did you get to Heaven? What's it like? Was it worth the trip?"

Zakkai scratched his head. "I got to Heaven. Was it worth the trip? To tell you the truth—I'm not sure. I don't know what to make of it. Heaven is just like Chelm. If I didn't know I was in Heaven, I would have thought I was back here. Everything's the same."

"Everything?" Adam and Eve asked.

"Everything!" said Zakkai. "Even the mudholes in the street."

"With all those angels hanging around, you'd think they'd at least have fixed the street," said Zelig.

"I didn't see any angels," said Zakkai. "If I did, they look like us."

Bayla Shayna let out a great sigh. "All my life I've been looking forward to going to Heaven. Now I find that it's just like Chelm. Is that all? Then what's the point of living?"

That's when Rabbi Devora spoke up. "Don't you see? That is the point! What did you think Heaven was? Marble palaces? Riding around in golden carriages? Angels waiting on you hand and foot? That's a fool's Heaven! What is Heaven? It's home. It's family. It's the kindness of people you see every day. Where is Heaven? You don't have to go far. Look around you. We make our own Heaven on earth. It's right here in Chelm."

Since that day the people of Chelm have been convinced that not only does Heaven look like Chelm, but Chelm actually is Heaven, muddy streets and all. Are they foolish? Perhaps.

Or perhaps the real fools are the people who laugh at them. Perhaps the story of the angel and the sack of souls really is true. The people of Chelm may be the wisest souls of all.

Author's Note

Where is Chelm? Is it a real place? Why are there so many stories about it? Where did they come from?

People are surprised to learn that Chelm is a real city in Poland. Jewish people have lived there since the fourteenth century. In 1939, on the eve of World War II, at least fifteen thousand Jewish people lived in Chelm, making up half the city's population. The real Chelm was a center of commerce, study, and scholarship, with a highly respected yeshiva.

So how did it come to be known as a town of fools?

No one knows.

Stories about towns of foolish people can be found in many cultures. Ancient Greeks had Abdera. The city of Gotham plays the role in English folklore. The Germans had the town of Schildberg. Schildberg may be the original source of the Chelm tales. A collection of Schildberg stories was translated into Yiddish in 1597. Various books appeared over the years connecting foolishness with other towns. The first collection of *Khelem Mayntses* (Chelm stories) appeared in 1867. The foolish tradition stuck to Chelm and led to an important Jewish literary tradition: the Chelm story.

I. L. Peretz, Sholem Aleichem, and Isaac Bashevis Singer, three of the most famous and beloved Jewish writers, all wrote Chelm stories. The earliest, and possibly the best-known, children's version of Chelm stories in English is *The Wise Men of Helm* by Solomon Simon, originally published in 1942 and still in print to this day.

Some readers may be surprised to encounter a woman rabbi and people of color in a Chelm story. That would have been highly unusual in Eastern Europe of the time, and the original Chelm stories reflected their time. So should ours. After all, no race, religion, nationality, or gender has a monopoly on foolishness.